S0-ADI-691

HELEN V. GRIFFITH

Grandaddy's Stars

PICTURES BY
JAMES STEVENSON

GREENWILLOW BOOKS NEW YORK

Watercolor paints and a black pen were used for the full-color art. The text type is Perpetua.

a division of William Morrow & Company, Inc., 1350 Avenue of the Americas, New York, NY 10019. Printed in Hong Kong by South China Printing Company (1988) Ltd.

First Edition 10 9 8 7 6 5 4 3 2 1

LIBRARY OF CONGRESS
CATALOGING-IN-PUBLICATION DATA

Griffith, Helen V.
Grandaddy's stars / by Helen V. Griffith ; pictures by James Stevenson.
p. cm.
Summary: Janetta's Grandaddy lives on a farm with chickens and a mule, and when he comes to visit her in Baltimore, Janetta is worried that he'll find the city boring.
ISBN 0-688-13654-0.
ISBN 0-688-13655-9 (lib. bdg.)
[1. Grandfathers—Fiction.
2. City and town life—Fiction.]
I. Stevenson, James (date), ill. II. Title.
PZ7.G8823Gs 1995 [E]—dc20
94-4113 CIP AC

In memory of Ed Strickland

—H. V. G.

For Walker and Jenny

—J. S.

CHAPTER ONE

"Company's coming," Momma said.

Janetta stopped playing with Star and looked up. "Who?" she asked.

Momma smiled and said, "Somebody from Georgia."

Janetta stared at Momma. Star patted Janetta's knee to make her play some more, but Janetta just kept staring at Momma. "Grandaddy lives in Georgia," she said.

"I know he does," said Momma.

"But he doesn't travel much," Janetta said.

"Not a whole lot," Momma agreed.

"It's hard for him to get away," Janetta said, "because he has a mule to take care of."

Momma nodded. "He does have a mule."

"Then there's the chickens," Janetta said, "and the cat."

"That cat can take care of herself," Momma said, "and he found somebody to tend the livestock."

Janetta jumped up and threw herself on her mother. "It *is* Grandaddy!" she yelled.

Star scooted under the couch, and Momma laughed. "He'll be here tomorrow," she said. "And what are you trying to do, break every rib I've got?"

CHAPTER TWO

Janetta lay in bed and thought about what fun tomorrow would be.

"You'll have fun, too," she told Star. "You haven't seen Grandaddy since you were a little kitten."

Janetta wondered if Grandaddy was excited about the visit. Maybe he's too excited to sleep, she thought. Then he'll fall asleep when it's time to get up. Then he'll miss the train.

Janetta jumped out of bed. She ran into Momma's room and shook her awake. "I'm worried," she said.

Momma hid her face in her pillow. "I knew I shouldn't have told you ahead," she said.

Janetta shook Momma again. "I'm afraid Grandaddy won't be able to sleep, and he'll miss the train," she said.

"If he can't sleep, he'll be early for the train," Momma told her.

"But what if he's so tired on the train, he sleeps right through Baltimore?" Janetta asked. "What if he doesn't wake up until Philadelphia?"

"He'll like Philadelphia," Momma said. "He can visit the Liberty Bell."

Janetta was pretty sure Momma was teasing, but she couldn't help starting to cry.

Momma rolled over and turned on the light. "The last thing in the world that Grandaddy would do is miss that train," she said.

As soon as Momma was good and awake, Janetta felt better. "I wrote down all my plans for Grandaddy's visit," she said. "I'm going to show him everything in Baltimore."

Janetta ran to her bedroom and got her list. Then she ran back and jumped into bed with Momma. Momma took the paper and looked at it. It said:

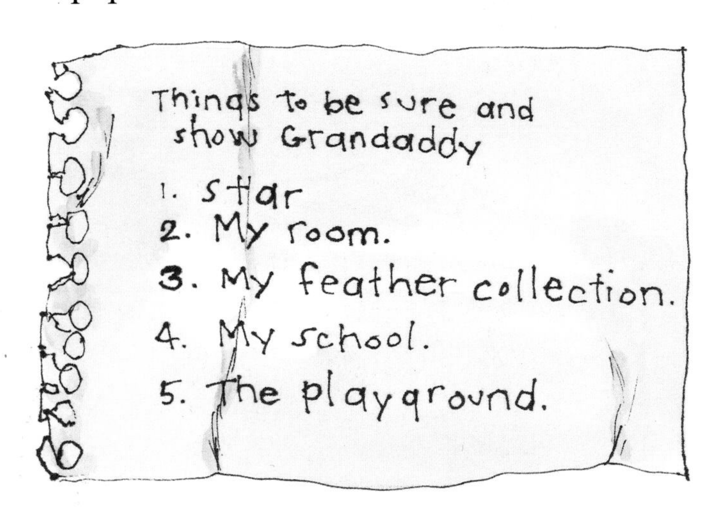

Things to be sure and show Grandaddy

1. star
2. My room.
3. My feather collection.
4. My school.
5. The playground.

Momma said, "Is this all you can think of in Baltimore to show Grandaddy?"

"I just wrote down the most important things," Janetta said.

Momma put down the list and turned off the light. She lay back and shut her eyes.

"Momma," Janetta said.

"Now what?" Momma said.

"I was just thinking," Janetta said. "What if the mule gets sick?"

"It won't get sick," Momma said.

"Well, what if it just pretends to be sick so Grandaddy won't leave?" Janetta said.

Momma turned her head and looked at Janetta. "Is it a tricky mule?" she asked.

Janetta thought about the mule. "No, it's not tricky," she decided.

"Well, then," Momma said, closing her eyes.

Janetta lay still for a few minutes. Then she said, "Momma."

"What now?" Momma said with her eyes closed.

"What if Grandaddy gets here, and he doesn't like it?" Janetta said.

"You're here, aren't you?" asked Momma.

"Yes," said Janetta.

"Then Grandaddy will be just fine," Momma said.

Janetta felt a lot less worried. She was even feeling a little sleepy. Then Star jumped up on the bed, looking for somebody to play with.

"Shhh. Don't wake up Momma," Janetta whispered.

But Momma was awake. "Is this the only bed in this house?" she asked.

Janetta giggled. "The only one with anybody in it," she said.

"I don't know what kind of a night's sleep Grandaddy is having," Momma said, "but I'll bet he's doing better than we are."

CHAPTER THREE

Janetta and Momma were at the railroad station waiting for Grandaddy's train.

While they waited, Janetta looked over her list of things to show Grandaddy. Last night she had thought it was a good list. Now everything on it sounded boring. Janetta started to worry. Grandaddy isn't going to like it here, she thought.

Just then they saw the train coming, and Janetta forgot about her list. When Grandaddy stepped off the train, she ran to him.

"Grandaddy!" she yelled. "You're really here!"

"Was there a doubt?" Grandaddy asked.

"She was afraid you'd oversleep and miss the train," Momma said.

"Nobody oversleeps with a yard full of chickens," Grandaddy said.

"Then she was afraid you'd sleep through your stop," Momma said.

"No chance of that," Grandaddy said. "I had to make sure the engineer didn't make any wrong turns and get us lost."

"Trains don't get lost, Grandaddy," Janetta said.

"Not with me watching them," said Grandaddy.

"Well, let's get along home," Momma said. "Janetta has a whole list of things to show you."

That made Janetta start worrying again. Her list was boring. Grandaddy wasn't going to like it here.

CHAPTER FOUR

Star was waiting for them at the door. He was at the top of Janetta's list of things to show Grandaddy.

Now Janetta thought, He's just an ordinary-looking cat. Grandaddy won't care about him.

Then Star meowed, and Grandaddy stopped and stared. "Can this handsome cat be the kitten with the same name as my mule?" he asked.

"He's not as cute as he was," Janetta said.

"What do you mean?" Grandaddy asked. "That is a fine-looking cat. That cat could win first prize in a show. He could go on the stage."

Janetta looked Star over carefully and decided that Grandaddy was right. "But he's still just a cat," she said, "not a mule like your Star."

Grandaddy picked Star up and sat down with him on his lap. "In a way this is better than my Star," he said. "When I try to hold my Star on my lap, we just can't get comfortable."

"Grandaddy," Janetta said, "your Star is a mule. Mules are too big for laps."

Grandaddy thought for a minute. "You may have something there," he said.

"Why don't you show Grandaddy around while I fix us something to eat?" Momma said.

Janetta didn't want to show Grandaddy around. There was nothing interesting to see. At Grandaddy's place there were chickens on the porch, and from the windows you could look out at the vegetable patch and the railroad track. Here you just saw buildings.

But Momma said, "Go on," so Janetta took Grandaddy to her room, because that was next on her list.

Grandaddy stood in the doorway and looked.

He thinks it's boring, Janetta thought.

Suddenly Grandaddy said, "What do you know!" and he hurried to the window.

Janetta followed him. "What is it?" she asked.

"That's the same patch of sky I see from my room in Georgia," Grandaddy said.

Janetta looked at the sky. "How can you tell?" she asked.

"By the stars," Grandaddy said. "Those stars are my own stars. They're glad to see me, too."

Janetta looked at the stars. She couldn't tell whether they looked glad or not. "How do they know you, Grandaddy?" she asked.

"We've been looking at each other for a long time," Grandaddy said.

Janetta looked some more. She began to think that maybe the stars did look glad to see Grandaddy, at that. "They don't know me at all," she said.

"Give them a wave," Grandaddy said.

Janetta waved, and then she stared very hard into the sky. "I don't think they waved back," she said.

"They will," Grandaddy said. "You just took them by surprise."

"Is anybody hungry?" Momma called, and Janetta and Grandaddy headed for the kitchen.

"Momma," Janetta said, "did you know that Grandaddy and I have the same stars?"

"I didn't know," Momma said, "but I'm not surprised."

CHAPTER FIVE

At breakfast the next morning Momma told Grandaddy, "Janetta's got plans. You're going to have a busy day."

"That'll be a change," Grandaddy said. "I haven't had a busy day since the chickens decided to fly south for the winter."

"How did that keep you busy, Grandaddy?" Janetta asked.

"Well, I didn't want them to go," Grandaddy said. "But no sooner did I grab one than another would take off."

"But Grandaddy," Janetta said, "didn't you tell them that they were already pretty far south?"

"Chickens are hard to talk to," Grandaddy said, "especially when they're stirred up. If that grasshopper hadn't come along, they'd have been gone."

Janetta laughed. "What could a little grasshopper do?" she asked.

"When the chickens saw the grasshopper, they all thought, Snack!, and their traveling plans went right out of their heads," Grandaddy told her.

"Oh, Grandaddy," Janetta said, "did they eat him?"

"They chased him all over the yard," Grandaddy said, "but he was an extra lively grasshopper."

"He got away," Janetta said happily.

Grandaddy nodded. "Last time I saw him, he was headed for the high weeds," he said. "He looked worn out, but I think he enjoyed the excitement."

"I thought you two were going sightseeing," Momma said. "Where's your list, Janetta?"

Janetta took the list out of her pocket. She took a pencil and crossed off "Star" and "my room."

"What's next?" Grandaddy asked.

Janetta read, "My school."

It was really "feather collection," but Janetta had decided to skip that.

With all those chickens around, Grandaddy sees plenty of feathers, she thought. He won't care about my collection.

But when they stood in front of her school building, it didn't seem any more interesting than the feathers.

“It’s ugly,” Janetta said.

“It’s not ugly, just serious-looking,” Grandaddy said. “It looks like a place where you learn important things. It looks like a place where future Presidents go to school.”

“It’s just a school for everyday people,” Janetta said.

“That’s hard to believe,” Grandaddy said. “If I’d gone to that school, I don’t doubt that I’d be President right this minute.”

“Presidents have a lot to do,” Janetta said.

Grandaddy nodded. “Might have to put in another phone,” he said.

“Grandaddy, you couldn’t stay home if you were President,” Janetta said. “You’d have to go and live in the White House.”

Grandaddy raised his eyebrows. “Is that the law?” he asked.

“I don’t know,” Janetta said, “but all the Presidents do it.”

Grandaddy thought it over. “Well, I guess it would be all right for a few years,” he said. “That mule likes a change now and then.”

“Grandaddy,” Janetta said, “I don’t think the mule would like the White House.”

"Why not?" Grandaddy asked. "Yard too small?"

"I think there's enough yard," Janetta said, "but there's probably not a shed."

"There must be a shed," Grandaddy said. "Where else would the chickens sleep?"

"I don't think Presidents have time for chickens," Janetta said.

"No time for chickens!" Grandaddy said. "Well, it's a good thing I didn't go to that school. It would have caused me all kinds of trouble when I got to be President."

"Grandaddy, you're kidding, aren't you?" Janetta asked.

"Half," said Grandaddy. "What's next on that list?"

Janetta didn't have to look. "The playground," she said.

But when they got to the playground, Janetta wondered why she had put it on her list. It was just a weedy empty lot with newspapers blowing around in it.

Grandaddy stood and looked at the playground. "I want to remember it so I can describe it to the mule," he said. "This is the very kind of place that mule would like."

"It's just a boring empty lot," Janetta said.

"Just right for running," Grandaddy said. "No worry about stepping on pea plants or chickens or a kitten. That mule loves to run."

"I do, too, Grandaddy," Janetta said. She ran all the way across the playground and back to Grandaddy. "It *is* just right for running," she said. "Be sure and tell the mule."

When they got home, they told Momma where they had been, and Momma said, "Baltimore is an interesting city. Tomorrow we'll do some real sightseeing."

"That'll be fine," Grandaddy said, "but I've seen the best places already."

CHAPTER SIX

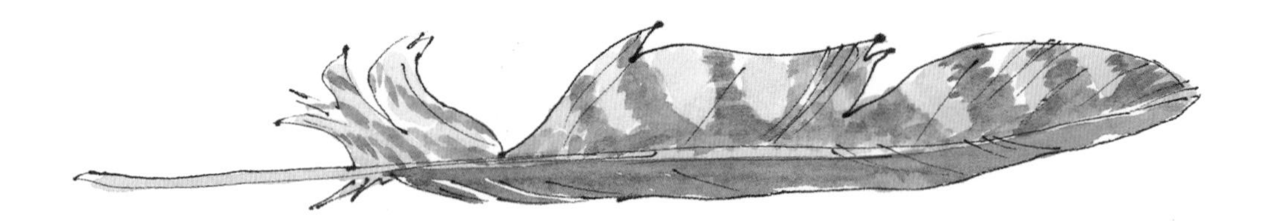

Grandaddy and Janetta were at Janetta's window looking at the stars.

Janetta waved, and then she waited. "They still didn't wave back," she said.

"Give them time," said Grandaddy.

Janetta and the stars looked at each other a little longer, and then she said, "Grandaddy, there's one more thing on my list of things for you to see." She took a box from her bookcase and handed it to him.

He opened it and looked inside. "Feathers," he said.

"I guess you see enough feathers at home," Janetta said. She was sorry she had brought out her collection.

But Grandaddy said, “Not like these.” He looked carefully at the feathers, one by one. “These feathers have traveled,” he said. “These feathers have stories to tell.” He took a bright black feather from the box. “This one, for instance.”

“I picked it up on the playground,” Janetta told him.

“Well,” Grandaddy said, “this could be a feather from the very bird that almost talked my chickens into leaving home.”

“Really, Grandaddy?” Janetta asked. She examined the feather. “I think it’s from a starling,” she said.

“It was a starling that was talking to my chickens,” Grandaddy said. “They would all look over at me, and then they would whisper together.”

“I didn’t know birds could whisper,” Janetta said.

"They can do it," Grandaddy said. "They just don't do it much." He gave the box back to Janetta. "I don't recognize anybody else," he said, "but there are a lot more stories there."

"Only I don't know what they are," Janetta said.

"What you don't know," said Grandaddy, "you make up."

Janetta took the starling feather out of the box. "This is for you, Grandaddy," she said. "If you see the starling again, you can tell her she dropped it."

"I will," Grandaddy promised. "But I'll lock up the chickens first."

CHAPTER SEVEN

The day Grandaddy went home, Janetta didn't feel right all day. She didn't feel like playing, but she didn't feel like sitting still, either.

"I think I'm sick," she told Momma.

"You just miss Grandaddy," Momma said.

"What's the use of having company, if you're going to feel so bad when they leave?" Janetta asked.

"Just think about the fun you had," Momma said, so Janetta sat and thought.

"I showed Grandaddy everything on my list," she said.

"That's good," Momma said.

"He said my school looked like a President's school," Janetta said.

Momma smiled. "Why don't you prove him right?" she said.

"He thinks Star could go on the stage," Janetta said.

"That would be fine with me," Momma said.

"And Grandaddy said the mule would love the playground," Janetta said.

"No mule visitors," said Momma.

That made Janetta laugh, and laughing made her feel better. She pulled Star onto her lap and kissed his ears.

"I'm glad you're not a mule," she said, and Star seemed glad of it, too. He sat and purred while Janetta made up feather stories for him and Momma.

When bedtime came, Janetta went to her window and waved at the stars before she got into bed.

Momma came in to kiss her goodnight, and she said to Janetta, "What's that big smile all about?"

"It's about Grandaddy's stars," Janetta said, pointing toward the window. She and Momma looked out at the little lights shining in the sky. "If Grandaddy's looking at them tonight," Janetta said, "he just saw every one of them wave."